Lucky Lions,

We want to wish you best of luck in Kindergarten.

Keep reading , adding and growing your brain.

We will miss you but know you are on a path to greatness.

Love,

Miss Delli

Miss Lindsay

Michael Brown

MULCH
The Lawnmower

Written and Illustrated by
SCOTT NELSON

ɷ

KRBY Creations, LLC
Bay Head, New Jersey
www.KRBYCreations.com

Dedicated to
Ginny and Collin

Visit

www.MulchtheLawnmower.com
for updates, free coloring pages, and other fun items.

ೠ

ISBN-10   0-9745715-4-7
ISBN-13   987-0-9745715-4-6
Library of Congress Control Number: 2005921144

Printed and Bound in China

Editor and Publisher:
Kevin R. Burton
KRBY Creations, LLC
Post Office Box 327
Bay Head, NJ 08742
www.KRBYCreations.com

Inside a small, comfortable garage, were two lawn mowers. The first was a red sit-down mower named Rider while the second was a yellow walk-behind mower named Mulch. On every work day, Mr. Corey would load Rider onto a trailer and take him to cut grass at a professional baseball stadium. Mulch would sit at the garage door and sadly watch the pair leave.

You see, Mulch and Rider were close friends, and Mulch never let his desire to do Rider's great job stop him from being proud of his friend. In fact, Mulch always made a point of yelling out words of encouragement as they drove off to the baseball stadium. "Have an awesome day Rider! No one can do a better job cutting grass than you!" "Thanks Mulch! Have a good day yourself!" Rider yelled back as he would rumble off down the road and out of view.

Once they were gone, Mulch would sigh. It was Mulch's job to cut the Corey family's yard but he was certain it couldn't compare to cutting the grass of a baseball stadium. "It must be just wonderful," Mulch thought. In fact, Rider had told him that baseball grass was always extra green, always extra soft, and a lot easier to cut than the lawn at the Corey's home.

Later one day Mr. Corey's wife came out to the garage to get some gardening tools. She noticed Mulch sitting near the garage door looking lonely. "Why Mulch, you look so sad," she said. "I bet you miss your friend Rider. I know Mr. Corey and I miss each other an awful lot each day as well. It just seems that the both of them are always at work.

Then Mrs. Corey said, "Hmm, maybe I can talk Mr. Corey into taking you with them someday. I bet they could teach you how they cut grass at the baseball stadium. Maybe you could even cut a little yourself. Of course that means you'll have to be ready. We could get you some extra practice in our own yard. How does that sound?" Mrs. Corey patted Mulch on the engine and then left the garage to start her own gardening. Mulch was excited by what Mrs. Corey had just said. If the time ever did come to help Mr. Corey and Rider at the baseball stadium, Mulch knew that he'd have to be prepared.

Mulch decided to work twice as hard to prove that he was good enough for the job. He'd always cut perfectly straight lines in their grass at home and Mulch had always tried to catch every bit of the grass clippings in his bag. He wanted Mr. Corey to be proud of him. One of the proudest moments for Mulch was when he once rode on two wheels to avoid hitting a hose and water sprinkler hidden in some deep grass. "WOW!" said Mr. Corey as he patted Mulch's engine. "Good Job Mulch. I never saw it." Mulch was very proud of himself that day.

At the end of each day, Mr. Corey would back up the driveway and unload Rider into his spot in their garage. He checked his oil and filled him back up with gas. He cleaned out Rider's air filter and washed off all the baseball dust and dirt that had built up after their hard day. Once Mr. Corey was done he'd head inside for dinner. Mulch always had a hundred questions for Rider. Even though Rider was tired, he would always take the time to answer all of Mulch's questions.

"Well," said Rider. "The baseball players were very kind to me today and complimented my cutting job around the pitcher's mound. In fact, the team's best pitcher gave me a new nickname — Big Red! He even asked for a ride out to the bullpen." "Wow!" Mulch thought. These stories always sounded so great. He just knew that some day he had to see the baseball stadium for himself.

The next day, the morning started off as usual. Rider left with Mr. Corey and Mulch sat bored and lonely near the garage door. When Mr. Corey and Rider came back to the garage later that night however, things had changed. Rider looked sick. He looked extra dusty and tired. Every time Mr. Corey tried to start him up, Rider would only cough and blue smoke would come out of his engine.

Mr. Corey worked on Rider's engine for a long time but Rider still wasn't working right by the time Mr. Corey shut the garage door for the night. "What's wrong?" Mulch said to his friend. "Gee," said Rider, "I don't know what happened to me. One minute I was in the outfield mowing along fine and then I just suddenly conked out." Mr. Corey said that he'd have to wait until tomorrow morning before he could order me a new part. He said I'm missing something from my engine and he can't understand where it went. It might take a few days before I'm all better."

"A FEW DAYS!" Mulch exclaimed. "What about the big baseball game tomorrow night? The #1 team in baseball is coming to play us and Mr. Corey said that the grass has to be perfect. Who's going to finish cutting the grass so our team will be ready?"

"I don't know" sighed Rider. "Maybe you can do it for me." And with those words, Rider quickly drifted off to sleep.

Do it for you? Mulch thought. What was Rider talking about? I don't know how to cut baseball stadium grass. I'd need Rider there to show me how. This was nothing like the plan that Mrs. Corey and Mulch had talked about earlier.

Once he was inside, Mr. Corey told Mrs. Corey about the problem with Rider. "It seems like part of his engine is missing. Strangest thing. It's going to take me a few days to get a replacement part too. I don't know what I'm going to do now. Mulch is just too small to do such a large job."

Mrs. Corey sat down at the kitchen table with Mr. Corey. "Oh, give Mulch a chance. He's always done such a great job in our own lawn, I'm sure he'll do just fine at the baseball stadium."

Mr. Corey shrugged his shoulders and said, "OK honey. I'll give Mulch a chance but I really don't think he can handle this job."

That night Mulch had a difficult time getting much sleep. He'd thought all night about the various things that could go wrong if Mr. Corey indeed needed his help. His imagination really got carried away. "What if I'm mowing and I run over a base? Or what if I'm mowing and I accidentally fall into the dugout?" Soon it was morning and the garage door went up. Mr. Corey walked up to Mulch. "Rider's engine needs a new part, but it's going to take a few days to fix him up. Mulch, I really need your help today at the stadium." Mulch gulped!

Mr. Corey started to get Mulch ready: he filled up his gas tank, installed a new spark plug, added some oil and wiped him down with a clean cloth. He then rolled him out to the trailer and tied him down securely so he wouldn't roll around while driving to the baseball stadium. Mr. Corey climbed into his truck. Just then, Rider woke up. "Hey," Rider sleepily yelled out. "Go get 'em Mulch. Good luck!" The trailer started pulling out of the driveway. Rider yelled out "Oh, one more thing — keep your eyes open for the ....."

But, Mulch couldn't hear the last thing that Rider had yelled out over the sounds of the truck. "What did you say? What was that?" Mulch yelled back, but they were already on their way.

The trip to the baseball stadium was very interesting. It had been a long time since Mulch had seen anything but the view from the garage. Eventually, Mr. Corey brought the truck and trailer to a stop in front of a gate. A security guard approached Mr. Corey and the two talked for a few minutes. Soon the guard walked back to the trailer and looked in at Mulch. "Hi Mulch," the guard said in a friendly tone. "Welcome to our baseball stadium. I just heard that you're filling in for Rider today while he's sick. I wish you luck — and thank you for joining our team." Mulch smiled. The guard said that he was on THE TEAM. Was he really? The gate then opened and Mr. Corey drove straight towards a strange tunnel.

Mulch had never been inside a tunnel before. But it didn't take long for them to travel through it and back into the daylight. It took a minute for Mulch's eyes to adjust to the sunlight again, but when they did Mulch was astonished at what he saw.

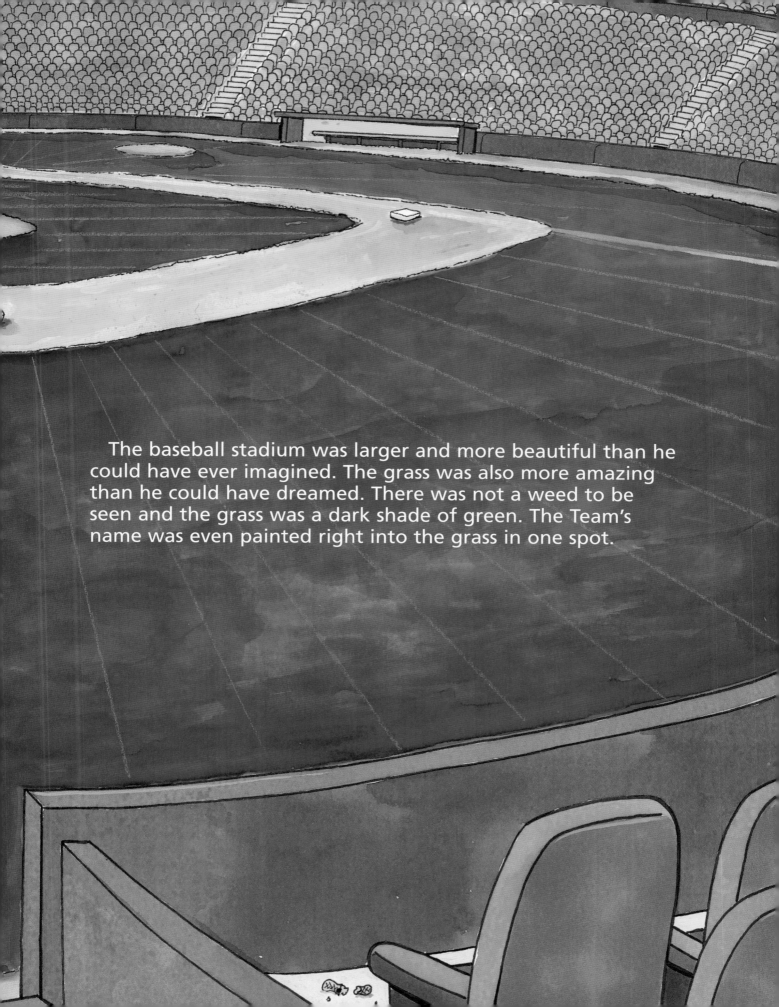

The baseball stadium was larger and more beautiful than he could have ever imagined. The grass was also more amazing than he could have dreamed. There was not a weed to be seen and the grass was a dark shade of green. The Team's name was even painted right into the grass in one spot.

Mr. Corey unloaded Mulch and pushed him to home base. Mr. Corey then knelt down next to Mulch and said, "OK Mulch, this is the Big League. I need you to cut the grass just like you do at our home. We'll start off with the infield and then we'll mow near the dugouts."

"Oh, I almost forgot," he said. "You can't cut grass at a Big League field without looking like a big league cutter." Mr. Corey then pulled out a team baseball cap and put it on top off Mulch's engine. "There you go" said Mr. Corey. "Now you even look like a Big League mower." And with that Mr. Corey started Mulch's engine and they were off.

The sun burned down on Mr. Corey and Mulch as they cut grass in all the different locations of the baseball stadium. Mulch was very thankful to have his new hat to shield his eyes from the bright sun. Back and forth. Back and forth. They cut the grass for hours. Suddenly, Mulch's eyes caught something in the grass and he had to swerve really hard to avoid running over it. In fact, he swerved so hard, he went up on two wheels just like he'd done before in the Corey's backyard.

Mr. Corey shut Mulch off quickly and yelled out "What was that all about?" Mulch was confused. He knew he had seen something in the grass but he wasn't sure what it was. He had just reacted. What if Mr. Corey was mad that he ruined his straight cutting lines? Mr. Corey walked back to the spot Mulch had swerved around and bent down to one knee. After a moment he stood up and walked back over to Mulch with something in his hand.

Mr. Corey was smiling. "Mulch, do you know what you swerved around back there? This is the missing part of Rider's engine. I don't know how you spotted this thing in the tall grass. Had one of the players stepped on this part while playing baseball, they'd have been hurt for sure. Great Job Mulch!"

Mr. Corey started Mulch back up and continued cutting the outfield grass. Mulch was so focused on what he was doing that he hadn't noticed that much of the baseball team had gathered around the dugout area and were watching them finish up. The news of what Mulch had done had traveled around the stadium. When they were finally done, Mr. Corey pushed Mulch over to the group of ball players. One of the players stepped forward and yelled "Ready Team?" Then all the baseball team yelled "Two- Four -Six - Eight, who do we appreciate? MULCH, MULCH, MULLLLLCH!!!!" Everyone then threw their baseball caps up into the air and they rained down all around Mulch like confetti.

The entire stadium grass looked great and after a long day, Mulch was very tired. Mr. Corey loaded Mulch back up onto the trailer, smiled and said "Mulch, I have to be honest with you. I really thought you were too small for this job. Who would have thought a little guy like you could handle such a big baseball field like this? You certainly proved me wrong." Mr. Corey then reached into his pocket for something and placed it on top of Mulch's cutting deck.

Mulch looked at what Mr. Corey had put on top of him and was shocked. It was an actual baseball. "Each game the coach of the team decides who deserves the Game Ball. The ball symbolizes a thank you to the player that's tried their hardest." Mr. Corey then said, "Mulch, you're the Most Valuable Player to the team and to me."

    As they began to head into the tunnel, Mulch looked back at the baseball team. Many of the players were waving good-bye to him. "See you tomorrow Little Yellow!" the team's star player yelled out. His own nickname. Wow! Mulch really wished he could come back tomorrow, but he knew this was his first and last chance to cut the grass at the stadium. This job was Rider's.

On the ride back to the garage, Mulch was so tired he fell right asleep. When the truck and trailer arrived back home, Mulch awoke to find Rider waiting for them in front of the garage door.

Once Mr. Corey had unloaded him and went into the house to visit with Mrs. Corey, Rider blurted out, "How did it go? Did you like it? Did any of the players talk to you?" Mulch excitedly answered all of Rider's questions. He told him about swerving around something in the grass and about his new "Little Yellow" nickname. Mulch then showed Rider the MVP ball. "Oh my gosh," Rider said. "They only give that ball out to real teammates. You must have done great."

The Corey's house door then opened and Mr. and Mrs. Corey
came out together. Mr. Corey was carrying the engine part in his
hand that Mulch had found on the field. He quickly went to work
bolting it back onto Rider's engine. Mrs. Corey started to talk.
"Mr. Corey told me all about what happened at the baseball field
today, Mulch, and we're both so very pleased. I knew you could
do it and we think we've come up with a new plan for cutting
the grass at the stadium."

"Our plan," Mrs. Corey said as she looked at Rider and Mulch, "is that both of you will go to the baseball stadium every day. You'll both share the work. In fact, I'm going to be helping too." Mrs. Corey said. "I'll drive Rider in the outfield and Mr. Corey will push Mulch in the infield and near the dugouts."

Mr. Corey finished installing the part that had fallen off the engine. Rider was now his normal self again. "Yep," said Mr. Corey. "Now we're a real grass-cutting team!"

Everything was perfect. Mr. and Mrs. Corey could spend more time together. Rider wouldn't have to work so hard everyday. And Mulch wouldn't be lonely in the garage all day. What a great plan! "OK," said Mr. Corey. "If we're a real team, then we need to have a real practice. Our own lawn needs cutting so let's go!" So the Coreys, Rider and Mulch all started to cut the lawn together.

That night, as Mulch went to sleep, he couldn't help but smile from wheel to wheel. All his dreams had come true, and it happened alongside his family and best friend. What could be better? Mulch knew that he'd hit a grand slam!